Feeling the blood drain from her face, she just stared.

"Whatever it is I did to you, it's the reason you decided you never wanted to marry. I drove you into a life of single motherhood."

Relief making her almost giddy, she maintained her stance.

Unable to believe her luck.

Wow, he couldn't have walked into that one any better.

She told him the absolute truth. "Yes, you did drive me into single motherhood," she confirmed, looking him straight—belligerently—in the eye.

"Tell me what I did."

She shook her head. "No way. You don't get to start building up different justifications in your head to cloud real memories with fiction when you do remember."

His brows raised, he studied her another second or two. Nodded. "Fair enough."

She thought they were done until he said, "But it was so bad that you were pregnant within three months?"

"I won't bore you with details, but I'm drawn to men who have great qualities but who make immoral choices in their personal lives."

"So it wasn't me?"